The Feathers

W9-AGB-713

Felicia Law

Illustrated by Claire Philpott

Coloured by Xact Studio

allegra

Bamboo, Velvet and Beak sit on their log in the middle of the rainforest, just as they always do...

'What are those things on
your head, Velvet? Those things
sticking up in the air?' asks Bamboo.

4

'They're feathers,' says Velvet. 'I found them. And I think they look good'.

'I don't know,' says Beak.
'Birds have feathers on their heads
and you're not a bird!'

'It's a headdress,' says Velvet.
'Some people wear headdresses.'
'They wear dresses?' says Bamboo.
'On their heads?'

9

'No, silly,' says Velvet. 'They wear headdresses as decoration when they sing and dance...'

'Or to make them look fierce when they fight,' adds Beak. 'Each feather marks a brave deed.'

'Well, those feathers belong to a bird who's lost them,' says Bamboo. 'Velvet should give them back.'

'But there are thousands of birds in this forest,' says Velvet. 'How will I find the right bird?'

'That's easy,' says Bamboo.
'Red feathers belong to red birds and blue feathers to blue birds.'

'Or to birds with lots of different colours - pink, green and orange too. These feathers could belong to anyone!' says Velvet

15

They hunt high and low for
the right bird, but all
they find are
more feathers...

...yellow ones, orange ones
and violet ones. They find
feathers that are blue
and purple and pink. 17

Soon they have too many
feathers to carry.
So they stick them on their heads.

The parrots watch them from high up in the trees.

'There go the warriors,' they squawk,
'all dressed up in our old feathers.'

21

'Let's show those noisy parrots how fierce and brave we are,' says Beak.

'Come on! Let's dance and sing
and wrestle and fight.'

But Bamboo and Velvet are tired
out from collecting feathers -
and have fallen fast asleep.

23

The stories in the 'Bamboo, Velvet and Beak' series
find the three animals sitting together, observing
the rainforest and the events that come
and go around them.

Other titles in the series:
The Daddy-long-legs; The Rainbow;
The Creeper; The Walk;
The Tree; The Lunch; The Flower;
The Furry Caterpillar; The Bird.

Copyright © 2007 Allegra Publishing Ltd. All rights reserved.
ISBN 978-1-906292-03-4
Printed in China